The Runaway Turkey

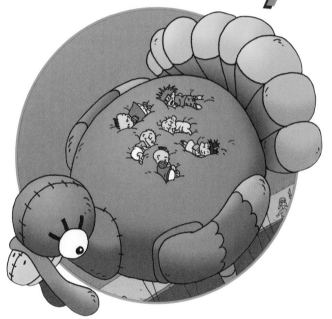

by Wendy Wax

illustrated by Larissa Marantz

and Shannon Bergman

Ready-to-Read

Simon Spotlight/Nickelodeon

New York   London   Toronto   Sydney   Singapore

Based on the TV series *Rugrats*® created by Arlene Klasky, Gabor Csupo, and
Paul Germain as seen on Nickelodeon®

SIMON SPOTLIGHT
An imprint of Simon & Schuster Children's Publishing Division
1230 Avenue of the Americas
New York, New York 10020

Manufactured in the United States of America
First Edition
2 4 6 8 10 9 7 5 3 1

Library of Congress Cataloging-in-Publication Data

Wax, Wendy.
The runaway turkey / by Wendy Wax.
illustrated by Larissa Marantz and Shannon Bergman
p. cm. — (Ready-to-read ; #13)
Summary: At the Thanksgiving Day Parade, the babies upstage Cornhusk
Princess Angelica when they arrive on top of a giant turkey balloon.
ISBN 0-689-85892-2
[1. Parade—Fiction. 2. Thanksgiving Day—Fiction.
3. Babies—Fiction.]
I. Marantz, Larissa,ill. II. Title. III. Series. IV. Rugrats (Series); #13.
PZ7.W35117 Ru 2003
[E]—dc21

"Get up, Mommy!"

Angelica hollered as she

shook her mother awake.

"Today is my big day!"

Angelica was so excited she could barely eat her waffles. Her class had a float in the Thanksgiving Day parade.

And Angelica was going to

sit on the throne.

She had been practicing

her royal wave all week.

Didi, Betty, and Kira found
a great spot at the parade.
"We are over here!" they called
to Charlotte and Angelica.

"I am in the parade!"

Angelica said bragging.

"Can we be in it too?"

Kimi asked.

"No way!" replied Angelica.

Tommy spotted a brown mat.

"What is that?" he asked.

"Something to jump on!"

Kimi cried. "Try it!"

They all started jumping.

Dil bounced into the air,

clapping and giggling

with each jump.

The babies played on the mat until they had tuckered themselves out. One by one they fell fast asleep.

While they slept, the brown
mat turned into a giant
turkey balloon!
The babies floated way up
into the sky.

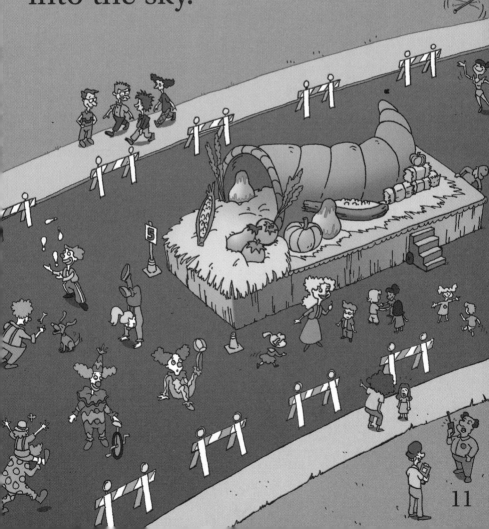

The parade was about to start.

Suddenly Angelica yelled,

"I have to go get my crown!"

"We do not have time," said

her teacher, Ms. Weemer.

12

When Ms. Weemer was looking

the other way, Angelica

climbed down from the float

and ran to find her mother.

"Sweetie!" cried Charlotte.

"What are you doing here?"

"My crown!" Angelica yelled.

Out of breath, she grabbed it

and dashed back to the float.

But she was too late.

The float had left

without her.

So Angelica caught a ride

on another float.

"Great, you are here!"

said a girl. "Put this on."

Being a big, fat turkey was *not* what Angelica had in mind! Someone plopped her on the table.

"Uh-oh!" Tommy shouted, waking the others. "We got kidnapped by a giant flying turkey during our nap."

"Maybe he got us mixed up
with his own babies.
He will probably take us
to a giant nest and sit on
us!" cried Lil.

"I see ants!" Lil exclaimed,

pointing to the crowd below.

"I think I am going to be sick,"

Chuckie said, covering his eyes.

"I know!" Tommy cried. "We
need to steer the turkey to
that tree and climb down it!"
"How do you steer a turkey?"
asked Phil.

Just then Dil saw a bird

and began to flap his arms.

"Good idea, Dil!" said Tommy.

"We can pretend we are birds

to steer the turkey. Flap!"

They flew closer and closer
to the tree and—*pop*!
Hissssssss. The giant turkey
balloon floated slowly
toward the ground.

"It is too late!" Kimi shouted.

"We are headed straight for

his giant nest!"

But the babies landed safely

on Angelica's class float . . .

right in her empty throne!

"Quick, Drew, get the camera," said Charlotte. "Here comes our little princess!"

"The crowd loves her!" said Drew.

But when the float pulled up,
all of the grown-ups gasped.
"How did our children get up
there?" asked Didi.

"I guess the big turkey went

to look for his real babies,"

said Tommy.

They waved at their parents.

"Angelica is a turkey!"

shouted Stu, pointing.

"Hey, who are you calling—"

began Drew, but then

he spotted Angelica.

When the parade was over,

Didi, Stu, Betty, Howard,

Kira, and Chas scooped

the babies up and gave them

lots of hugs and kisses.

Angelica climbed onto her
rightful throne.

"Okay, honey," called Charlotte.
"Let me see that royal wave
and smile!"

Happy Thanksgiving!